Goob
and
His
Grandpa

SEAN COVEY

Illustrated by Stacy Curtis

Ready-to-Read

Simon Spotlight
New York   London   Toronto   Sydney   New Delhi

To my precious daughter Rachel,
who lived a beautiful life.
I'm so looking forward
to our next trail ride.
—Sean Covey

In memory of Mark; you are missed.
—Stacy Curtis

SIMON SPOTLIGHT

An imprint of Simon & Schuster Children's Publishing Division

1230 Avenue of the Americas, New York, New York 10020

This Simon Spotlight edition August 2020

Copyright © 2013 by Franklin Covey Co.

For information about special discounts for bulk purchases, please contact Simon & Schuster Special
Sales at 1-866-506-1949 or business@simonandschuster.com.

Manufactured in the United States of America 0720 LAK

2 4 6 8 10 9 7 5 3 1

Library of Congress Cataloging-in-Publication Data

Names: Covey, Sean, author. | Curtis, Stacy, illustrator.

Title: Goob and his grandpa / by Sean Covey ; illustrated by Stacy Curtis.

Description: New York : Simon Spotlight, [2020] | Series: The 7 habits of happy kids | Audience:
Ages 5–7. | Audience: Grades K–1. | Summary: Goob's friends help him after his grandpa passes away.

Identifiers: LCCN 2019048898 | ISBN 9781534444645 (trade paperback)
ISBN 9781534444652 (hardcover) | ISBN 9781534444669 (eBook)

Subjects: CYAC: Grandfathers—Fiction. | Death—Fiction. | Grief—Fiction. | Friendship—Fiction.
Bears—Fiction. | Animals—Fiction.

Classification: LCC PZ7.C8343 Go 2020 | DDC [E]—dc23

LC record available at https://lccn.loc.gov/2019048898

Goob Bear and his grandpa
did everything together.
They collected bugs.
They went on long hikes.
They climbed trees and
ate honey out of beehives.
And they loved to wrestle
on the living room floor.
They loved each other very much.
They were best friends.

Goob didn't show up at school
on Monday morning.
Ms. Hoot said,
"Class, I'm really sorry to tell you
that Goob's grandpa died
yesterday."

"Goob won't be coming
to school this week.
Please try to cheer him up.
At times like this you
really need your friends,"
she explained to the class.

The gang got together at recess.
"That stinks. I bet Goob
misses him so much," said Lily.
"I think we should go see Goob,"
said Pokey.
"I don't know if he'll want to
see anyone right now. He is in
mourning," said Sophie.

"What would you want if your
grandpa died?" asked Sammy.
"I'd want my friends to be
with me," said Tagalong Allie.

Everyone showed up at Goob's
house after school that day.
Goob was sitting in his backyard.
He was crying.

Lily said, "Hi, Goob.
We came to see you because
we're really sad about your
grandpa."
"He was a really great guy,"
said Pokey.

"Thanks, Pokey. I'm sad too.
I don't know if I'll ever
be happy again," Goob said.
"If you're sad, then we're going
to be sad with you," said Jumper.

They all huddled around Goob,
and they were all sad together
for a long time.
When it was time for the gang to go
home, Goob felt a little better.

The next day everyone got together.
They made a plan.
They knew that Goob needed
friends, so each day after school,
one of them would visit Goob.

On Tuesday, Sammy and Sophie
showed up at Goob's house.
They had their walking sticks and
took Goob on a long walk
in the Far North Woods.
"That was refreshing," said Sophie.
"And fun, too," said Goob. "Grandpa
loved to walk in the woods."

On Wednesday,
Pokey took Goob on his boat.
They went to Fish-Eye Lake
and looked for bugs.

On Thursday, Lily and Tagalong Allie
helped Goob get some honey.
They climbed a tree
and found the beehive.
Lily was scared of the bees,
but Allie thought they were cute.

On Friday, Jumper agreed to have a
wrestling match with Goob
on his living room floor.
It wasn't much fun for Jumper
because Goob kept squishing him.

Still Goob had a great time,
so Jumper was happy.
Even Goob's mom didn't mind.

On Saturday, they all came
to visit Goob again.
"We brought you something,"
said Sophie.

"It's a honey-chocolate cake.
We made it ourselves. Don't worry.
We followed the recipe this time,"
said Lily.
"That's my favorite," Goob said.

"I made you a card, too,"
said Tagalong Allie.
Allie opened the card
and read it out loud.

The friends cut the cake.
They sat on the floor to eat it
and listen to Allie.

"Dear Goob,
I'm so sad your grandpa died.
He was your best friend.
Now Jumper and Pokey and Lily
and Sophie and Sammy and I
will be your best friends forever. . . .
I love you.
Allie."

Jumper started to cry, and Goob gave him a hug. "Thanks, Allie. That means everything to me. Thanks for being my friends, you guys. I'm going to miss my grandpa, but I don't feel so sad anymore," said Goob.

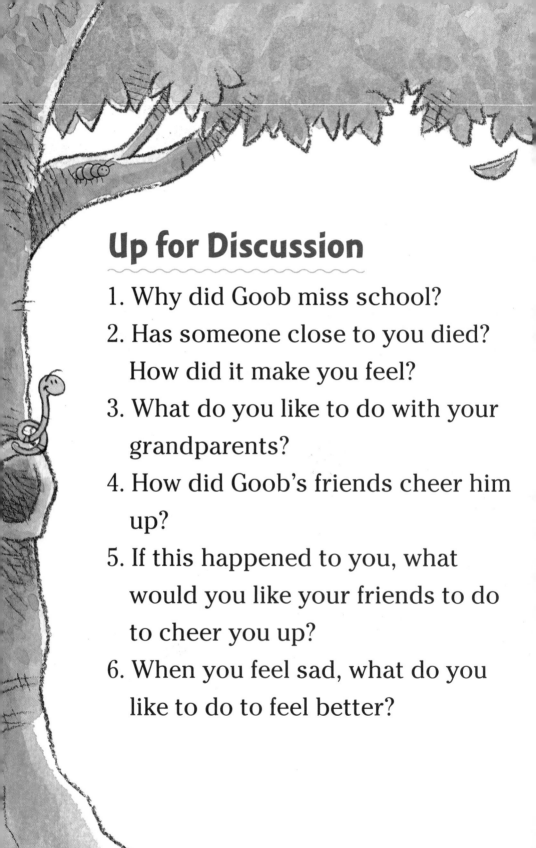

Up for Discussion

1. Why did Goob miss school?
2. Has someone close to you died? How did it make you feel?
3. What do you like to do with your grandparents?
4. How did Goob's friends cheer him up?
5. If this happened to you, what would you like your friends to do to cheer you up?
6. When you feel sad, what do you like to do to feel better?

Baby Steps

1. Write a note to someone you know who has had a family member or close friend or pet die.
2. Talk to your parents about what you can or will do when someone close to your family dies.
3. Go for a walk and look for beautiful things that make you happy.
4. Learn more about your family's history by talking to your parents and grandparents about your ancestors.

PARENTS' CORNER

I remember how shaken I felt when my father died. I knew I would never be the same. After his death, I thought spending time alone was what I needed, but surprisingly, I found just the opposite to be true. Spending time with family and friends is what helped me most. The whole ordeal reminded me, once again, that in the great scheme of things relationships are all that really matter. Everything else is fleeting. No one on their deathbed ever wished they'd spent more time at the office.

But it's so easy to forget that in this frenetic world of ours. We get so busy driving that we don't take time to get gas. We get so caught up in our work and our car pools and our to-dos that we forget to spend quality, face-to-face time with the living, breathing human beings all around us. That is why Habit 7, Sharpen the Saw, was invented. It reminds us to take time to renew, to unwind, to take a walk, to laugh, to cry, to step back and think deeply, and to invest in our most important relationships.

In this story, be sure to highlight what a difference Goob's friends made at this difficult time in his life. Often the best thing we can do when a friend or family member is hurting is just to say we're sorry and to mourn with them. We don't need to say anything or fix something; we just need to be there for them so they know we care. May we ever be willing to sharpen our saws by regularly spending time with the people we love, in both good times and bad.